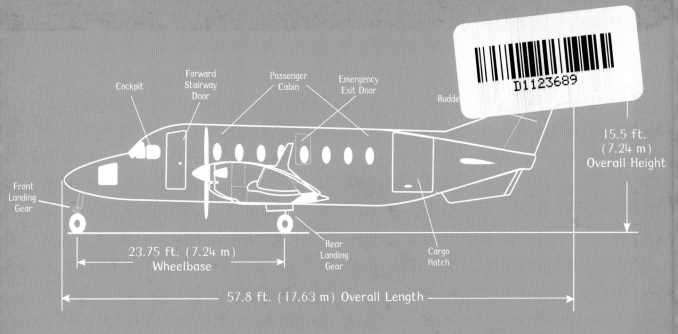

Cockpit

Forward Stairway Door

Passenger Cabin

Emergency Exit Door

Rudder

Front Landing Gear

Rear Landing Gear

Cargo Hatch

15.5 ft. (7.24 m) Overall Height

23.75 ft. (7.24 m) Wheelbase

57.8 ft. (17.63 m) Overall Length

Beechcraft 1900D
Regional Passenger Aircraft
Designed by Raytheon
Now owned by Textron
Wichita, Kansas

Capacity: 19 passengers
Cruising speed: 328 mph (528 kmh)
Range: 1,180 miles (1,900 km)
Max. altitude: 25,000 ft. (7,620 m)

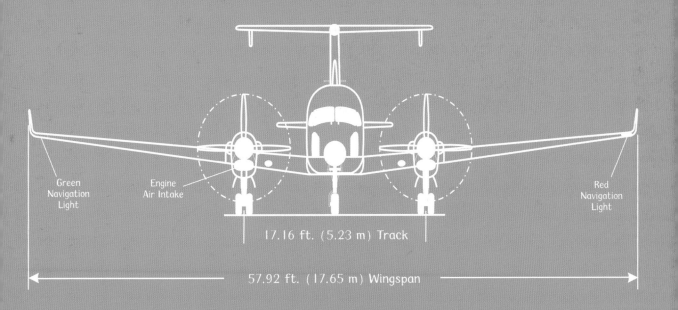

Green Navigation Light

Engine Air Intake

Red Navigation Light

17.16 ft. (5.23 m) Track

57.92 ft. (17.65 m) Wingspan

THIS BOOK
BELONGS TO

_____

Hi, Kids! I am Samantha Hedgehog, but you can call me Sammy. Join me to learn about how airplanes take off and land, and meet Harry and Pilot Stacey. Did you know about 22 million people fly somewhere every day? Pilots can learn to fly private airplanes, military jets, passenger or cargo planes, or helicopters, and some become astronauts and fly into space.

written by
Patrick T. McBriarty

illustrated by
Johanna H. Kim

CURLY Q PRESS
Books to Curl Up With

AIRPLANES
Take Off and Land

PTM
Werks Series

"I want to visit Grandma, but I'm a little afraid to fly." Harry says to his aunt Stacey.

"Don't worry, Harry, you will fly with me and see how everything works," Aunt Stacey says. "The wings of an airplane move through the air and create lift. At what we call 'takeoff speed,' the wings create enough lift for the entire airplane, passengers and all, to take off from the ground and fly. A pilot's job is to control the speed and direction of the airplane to safely take off, fly, and land. It's a special privilege to travel with a pilot, so you will have to be on your best behavior."

"Okay, I will," says Harry.

Inside the airport, passengers check in, check baggage, and pass through security before going to the gate to board their flight. Harry gets to check in through the special entrance and security check for pilots and crew with Aunt Stacey.

Harry and Aunt Stacey then go to the pilot's lounge.

STEP 1

THE FLIGHT PLAN. Before each flight pilots plan the flight path from start to finish and adjust altitudes and fuel for weather. The final flight plan is given to the air traffic controllers for approval, just as Pilot Stacey does for Crow-Flies Air Flight 6.

In the airport control tower, air traffic controllers clear aircraft for takeoff and landing, direct the movement of airplanes on the ground, and track in-flight aircraft on radar to keep everyone safe. Traffic control managers talk with other airport control towers to coordinate flights across the country.

Pilot Stacey and Harry pass through another security check and walk across the airport tarmac to the airplane.

STEP 2 | **CHECKS AND PREPARATION.** There are lots of things to do to get the airplane ready. Baggage handlers move luggage and packages from check-in to departing aircraft, and from arriving airplanes to baggage claim.

"Give Jackie your bag," Pilot Stacey tells Harry.
"She will load it onto the airplane."

Next, Pilot Stacey does the preflight inspection. She and Harry walk around the entire airplane checking the flaps, ailerons, rudder, elevators, and engines to make sure everything is ready before takeoff.

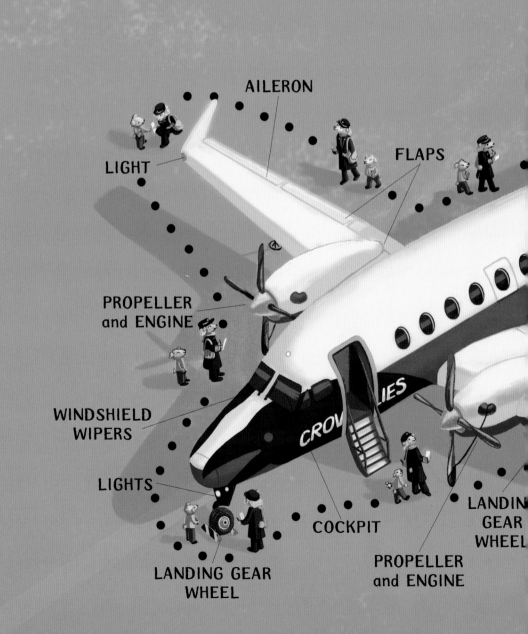

AILERON

FLAPS

LIGHT

PROPELLER
and ENGINE

WINDSHIELD
WIPERS

LIGHTS

LANDIN
GEAR
WHEEL

COCKPIT

PROPELLER
and ENGINE

LANDING GEAR
WHEEL

Mikey, the fuel truck driver, makes sure the airplane has enough fuel. He opens the fuel cap *snap-click,* and pulls the handle of the fueling nozzle. *Mmirr-rrurr* sings the truck's fuel pump as a gauge *ping-ping-ping* measures out the amount of fuel flowing into the airplane fuel tank.

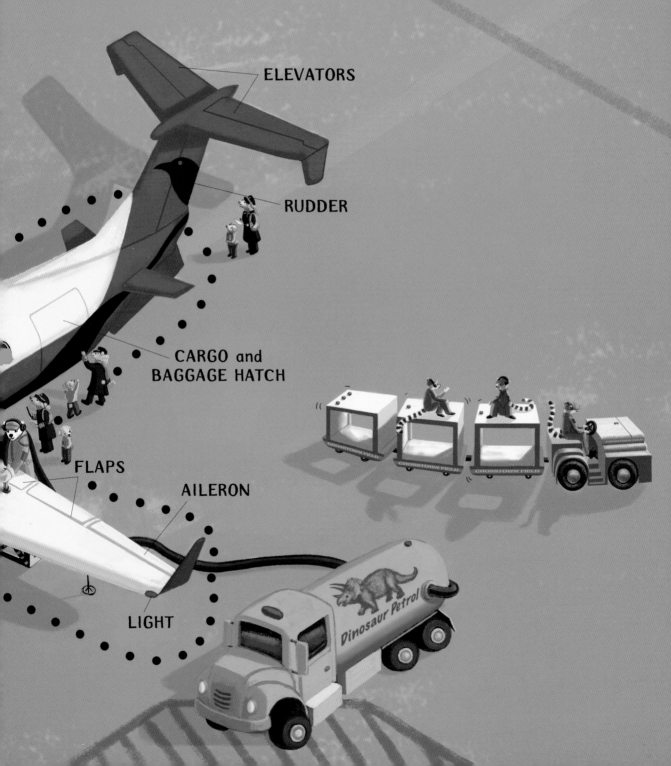

ELEVATORS

RUDDER

CARGO and
BAGGAGE HATCH

FLAPS

AILERON

LIGHT

Flight Attendant June has prepared the passenger cabin and greets everyone. "Welcome aboard, Captain Stacey! Copilot Schimer is already in the cockpit. And welcome aboard to you, too, Harry."

Pilot Stacey sits in the captain's seat. "Hello, Captain," says Copilot Schimer. "Hello, Harry, you can sit here in the jump seat. Please buckle up."

Pilot Stacey says, "Harry, I can answer any questions you have once we are in the air and the autopilot is on. Okay?"

"Okay, Captain," says Harry.

ON
OFF
Navigation Lights

Battery
Ready Left Right

On
Off
Engine
Start
Ready

41.6892"
37' 47.1612"
3ft

121.00
121.00

OFF ON

Copilot
Radio

Airspeed Indicator

300 50
250   100
200   150
0

Attitude Indicator

20 — 20
10 —10
10 —10
20 — 20

583
2
7
101 29.92
6 5 4
3

Altitude Indicator

Radar

Horizon
Indicator

20   20
15   15
15   15
20   20

Compass

30 33
W   N
24   3
21   6
S   E
18 15 12 9

Open

Close
Cockpit
Door

L   R

Turn
Coordinator

2 3 4
1
1,000 RPM
UP
DOWN
1
2 3

CABIN 0,000 ALT
PLANE 0,000 ALT

Cabin Pressure

Automatic
Direction
Finder

W   33
24   3
S   E

INSTRUMENTS
☑ Batteries on
☑ Radio
☐ Navi
☐
☐
gation

Landing
Gear

UP

DOWN

Rudder
Pedal

Propeller
Levers

FLAPS

DOWN

Left Right

Rudder

STEP 3

INSTRUMENTS. "Batteries on," Pilot Stacey says and flips a switch, *click*. "Check," says Copilot Schimer, tapping the gauge. The pilots talk back and forth. "Radio," *click*. "Check." "Navigation instruments," *click*. "Check." . . . *click*. "Check." . . . *click*. "Check." And so on until all the instruments and gauges are set and ready.

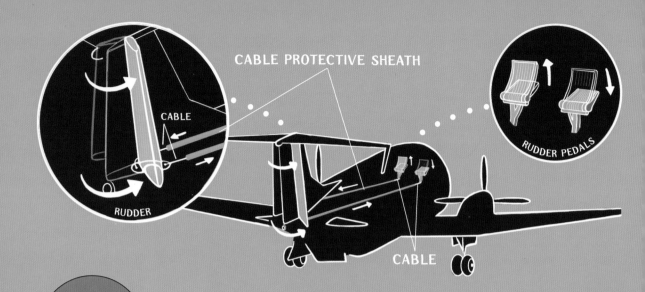

CABLE PROTECTIVE SHEATH

CABLE

RUDDER

RUDDER PEDALS

CABLE

STEP 4

CONTROL CHECKS. Pilot Stacey says, "Rudder left–right–neutral," pressing the foot pedals, *voomp-voomp-voov*. "Check, check, check," says Copilot Schimer, as the rudder moves left, right, and then to neutral.

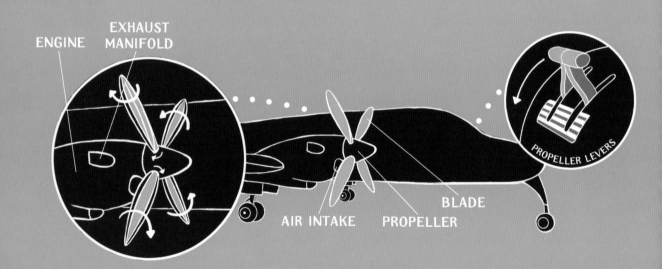

ENGINE

EXHAUST MANIFOLD

PROPELLER LEVERS

BLADE

AIR INTAKE   PROPELLER

Pilot Stacey says, "Pitch," testing the propeller pitch lever, *suomp-suomp*. "Check," says Copilot Schimer, seeing the angle of the propeller blades change. "Set for engine start," says Pilot Stacey, *suomp*. The propellers are angled for engine start. "Check," says Copilot Schimer.

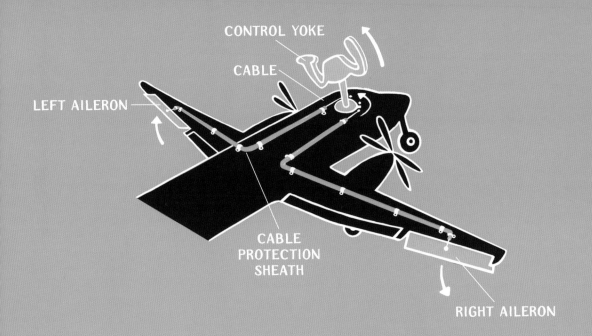

CONTROL YOKE

CABLE

LEFT AILERON

CABLE
PROTECTION
SHEATH

RIGHT AILERON

Pilot Stacey turns the control yoke, saying, "Left," *voomp*.
The pilots watch as the left and right ailerons move in
opposite directions to turn the airplane left while in flight.
Pilot Stacey turns the yoke saying, "Right," *voomp*. The
ailerons move in the other direction to turn the airplane to
the right while in flight. "Check, check," both pilots say.

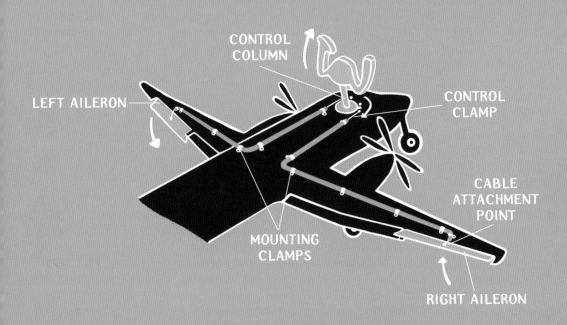

CONTROL
COLUMN

LEFT AILERON

CONTROL
CLAMP

CABLE
ATTACHMENT
POINT

MOUNTING
CLAMPS

RIGHT AILERON

With the pilots busy, Harry peeks out at
the cabin behind the cockpit to see . . .

STEP 5 **PASSENGERS BOARD.** Flight Attendant June helps passengers board the airplane, put away their bags, and take their seats.

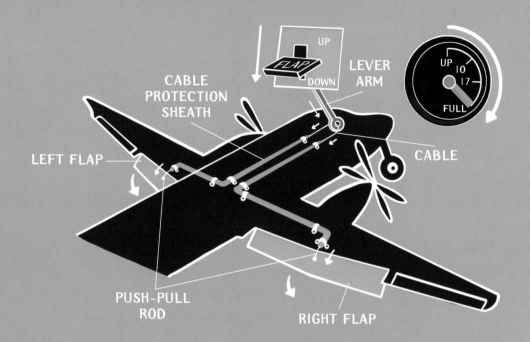

Back in the cockpit, Pilot Stacey says, "Flaps," pushing the lever down, up, down, *voomp-voomp-voomp*. Both pilots watch the flaps on each wing move down, up, down. "Check, check," they say.

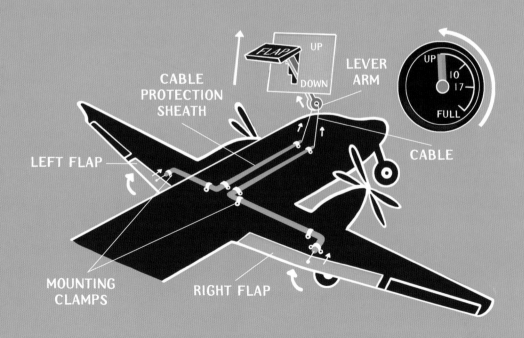

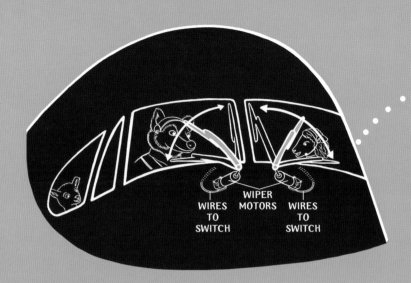

WINDSHIELD WIPERS

OFF
PARK
SLOW
FAST

WIPER
MOTORS

WIRES
TO
SWITCH

WIRES
TO
SWITCH

STEP 6

FINAL CHECKS. The pilots check the wipers, *click.* *Gromp-gromp-gromp,* the wipers croak, moving across the windshield. "Check." "Navigation lights," *click.* "Check." . . . *click.* "Check." . . . *click.* "Check." And so on until Copilot Schimer says, "A-OK. Pre-flight checklist complete, Captain."

ON
OFF
NAVIGATION LIGHTS

Pilot Stacey asks Flight Attendant June if the passenger cabin is ready. Flight Attendant June replies, "Everyone is aboard, seat belts are fastened, the hatch is closed, and the cabin is secure. Even Harry is buckled up. We are ready, Captain."

STEP 7

LEAVE THE GATE. Pilot Stacey pushes the engine throttles forward, *bbrroomm-bbrrroomm-bbroooomm*, releases the brakes, and taxis away from the gate, *brub-brub-brub*. She brings the airplane to a stop at the end of the runway and waits for clearance from the air traffic control tower.

STEP 8

CLEARANCE FOR TAKEOFF. Crosstown Field Air Traffic Controller Carrie spots Crow-Flies Air Flight 6 at the end of the runway. Seeing the runway clear and no airplanes approaching, she says into the radio, *(CRACKLE)* "Crow-Flies Air Flight 6, you are cleared for takeoff." *(CRACKLE)*

STEP 9   **TAKEOFF.** Pilot Stacey pushes the throttles all the way forward and power to the engines increases, *ggrrrOOOAAARRR!!* The brakes are released and the airplane increases speed, racing down the runway, *VVVRRROOOMMM!!!*

After reaching takeoff speed, Pilot Stacey says, "Rotate," and gently pulls back on the control yoke. The elevators on the tail wing angle up and the nose of the airplane rotates up as the airplane lifts off the runway, *SHHH-Whoooosh.*

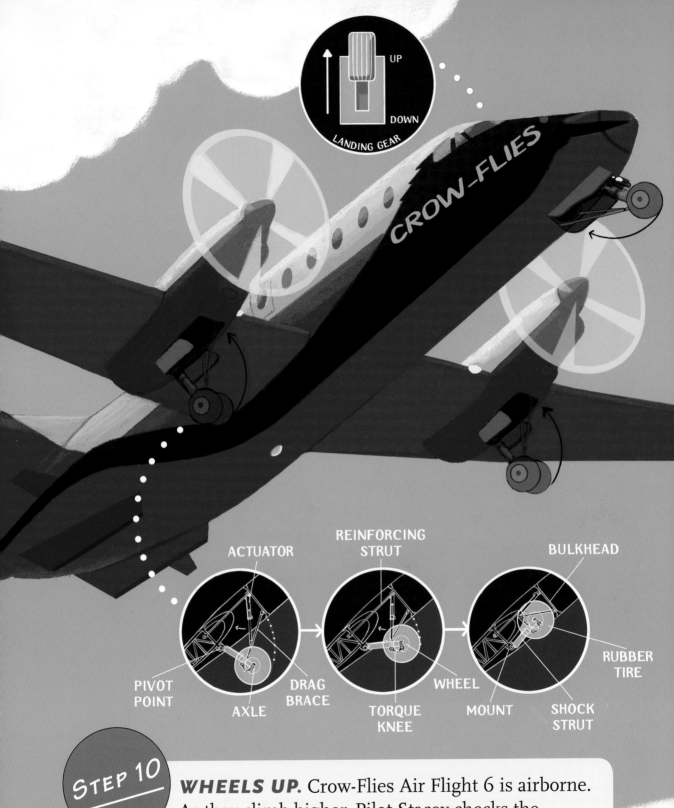

UP

DOWN

LANDING GEAR

CROW-FLIES

ACTUATOR

REINFORCING STRUT

BULKHEAD

PIVOT POINT

AXLE

DRAG BRACE

TORQUE KNEE

WHEEL

MOUNT

SHOCK STRUT

RUBBER TIRE

STEP 10

WHEELS UP. Crow-Flies Air Flight 6 is airborne. As they climb higher, Pilot Stacey checks the altimeter. "Positive rate of climb. Landing gear up," she says and switches the landing gear lever, *click*, and motors hum. *Thump-ca-lump*, the wheels fold into the airplane and the landing gear doors *clunk* shut.

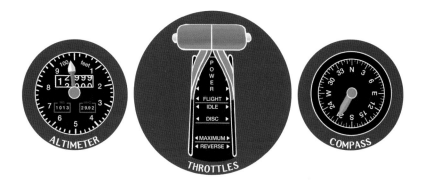

STEP 11

COME TO COURSE. Pilot Stacey guides the airplane to the proper altitude, levels off, and reduces the throttles to maintain cruising speed. As they continue, she gently turns the airplane, while checking the compass, to follow their flight plan.

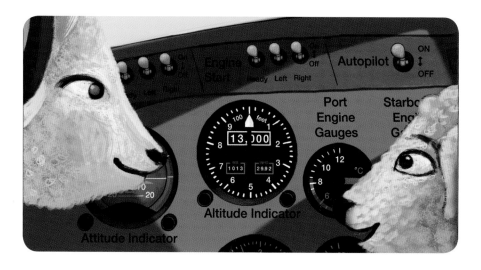

STEP 12

AUTOPILOT ON. Happy with the speed, altitude, and direction, Pilot Stacey says, "Autopilot," flips a switch, _click,_ and releases the controls. Automatically the airplane stays on course.

Copilot Schimer takes over checking instruments, looking for other aircraft and anything unusual as the airplane *whooshes* through the sky.

Harry asks, "Wow, are we really 13,000 feet off the ground?"

"Yes, according to the altimeter we are 13,000 feet above sea level. That is the cruising altitude from our flight plan, but this airplane could go twice as high if we had to," says Pilot Stacey.

They fly over many towns and cities on the way. Using the radio *(CRACKLE)*, Copilot Schimer checks in *(CRACKLE)* and out with the air traffic control towers whose air space they pass through along the way.

STEP 13

CLEARANCE TO LAND. Air Traffic Controller Harold, from the Bayside Landing control tower, gives Copilot Schimer wind and weather conditions and directions. "Crow-Flies Air Flight 6 (CRACKLE), turn left to compass heading one-eight-zero—you are cleared to land on Runway 18" (CRACKLE). Copilot Schimer repeats back the instructions so Air Traffic Controller Harold knows they were understood.

STEP 14 **AUTOPILOT OFF.** Pilot Stacey says, "Autopilot off," flips a switch, *click*, and takes over control of the airplane.

STEP 15 **LANDING APPROACH.** Pilot Stacey steers the airplane to compass heading one-eight-zero and begins their descent toward Bayside Landing's Runway 18.

Using the intercom, Pilot Stacey lets Flight Attendant June know they are on final approach. "Please prepare the cabin for landing."

A few minutes later, Flight Attendant June reports back, "All seat belts are fastened and the cabin is secure for landing."

On final approach, Pilot Stacey says, "Full flaps," and Copilot Schimer pushes the lever down. A motor hums as the flaps extend from the wings. The wind *whooshing* around the airplane gets louder, *SSHHHWHOOSH*. Later, Harry learns that extending the flaps down on the wings allows the airplane to fly slower, making it easier to land safely.

KURR-AR-RRR-LUNK!

UP
DOWN
LANDING GEAR

STEP 16

WHEELS DOWN. "Landing gear down," Pilot Stacey says and flips a switch, *click*. The hatch doors open, *whooshhh-sshhh*. Motors hum and *kurr-rr-rrr-lunk*, the landing gear is down, locked, and ready for landing.

STEP 17 **LANDING.** Nearing the runway, Pilot Stacey says, "Reducing throttle," and pulls back slightly on the throttle levers. Just before touchdown, she pulls back slightly on the yoke to flare the airplane.

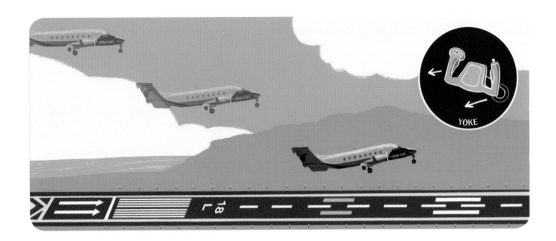

Flaring causes the nose of Crow-Flies Air Flight 6 to rotate up as it descends closer and closer to the ground. Seconds later, *eeerp-vvooorrrr,* the airplane's back wheels touch down on the runway tarmac.

As soon as the back wheels touch down, Pilot Stacey pushes the control yoke forward. The nose of the airplane rotates down, *eeerp-vvooorrrr,* and the front wheels touch down on the runway. Crow-Flies Air Flight 6 is now rolling down Runway 18 very fast. *VVRROOMMM.*

Pilot Stacey says, "Idle engines," and slides the throttle levers back. *Mmmrrruumm-humm,* sigh the engines. The *whoosh* of the wind around the airplane decreases quickly and the wheel brakes slow the airplane to taxi speed. Harry sighs, "Whew," realizing they are now safely on the ground.

GATES C1-C8

STEP 18

GO TO THE GATE. Pilot Stacey taxis the airplane, *brub-brub-brub,* toward the airport terminal and the waiting ground crew, who guide the airplane to a stop at the gate.

STEP 19   **ARRIVAL.** When the airplane comes to a complete stop at the Bayside Landing Airport, Flight Attendant June lets the passengers know it is now safe to move about the cabin but reminds everyone to be careful when opening the overhead bins.

STEP 20   **SHUTDOWN.** Copilot Schimer and Pilot Stacey do their postflight checks. "Shut down," she says, flips a switch, *click,* and the engines wind down to a stop, *VVVooorrrrvvv.* "Instruments on standby," *click.* "Check." "Radio off," *click.* "Check." . . . *click.* "Check." . . . *click.* "Check." And so on until Copilot Schimer says, "Shutdown is complete."

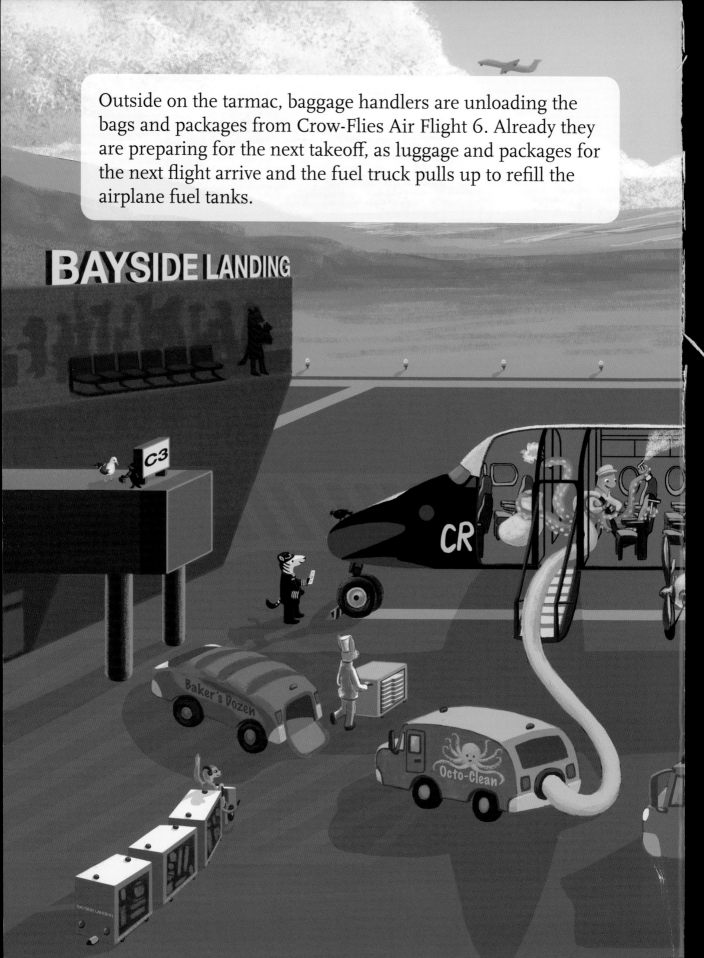

Outside on the tarmac, baggage handlers are unloading the bags and packages from Crow-Flies Air Flight 6. Already they are preparing for the next takeoff, as luggage and packages for the next flight arrive and the fuel truck pulls up to refill the airplane fuel tanks.

STEP 21

FLIGHT REPORT. Copilot Schimer, Pilot Stacey, and Harry file the flight report with the airline office.

As Aunt Stacey and Harry leave the airport terminal, she asks, "So, what did you think, Harry?"

Harry is so excited and full of questions, "Umm, great!?" is all he can manage to say.

Dinosaur Petrol

The Crow-Flies airplane will make several more flights today, and each pilot, copilot, and crew will follow the same twenty-one steps to take off and land.

At night, airplanes go into the airport hangars so mechanics can check fluids, make repairs, and perform routine maintenance so the airplanes are ready to go again the next morning. This happens over and over again, almost every day.

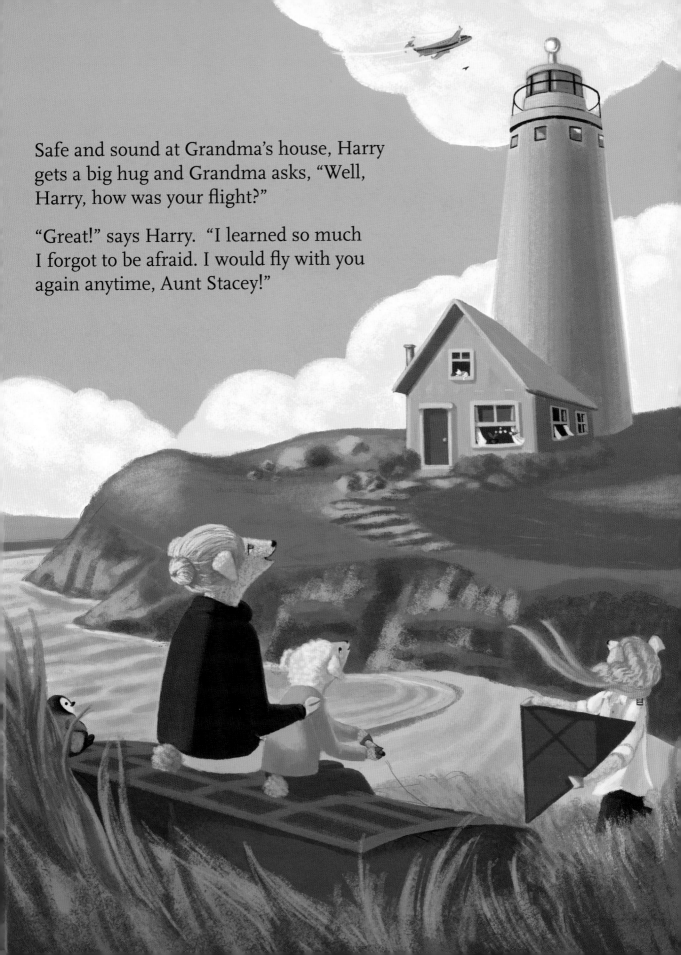

Safe and sound at Grandma's house, Harry gets a big hug and Grandma asks, "Well, Harry, how was your flight?"

"Great!" says Harry. "I learned so much I forgot to be afraid. I would fly with you again anytime, Aunt Stacey!"

AUTHOR'S DEDICATION:
To future pilots, air traffic controllers, flight and ground crews.
Special thanks to Chris Lynch, Lora Yowell, and Lionel Hawkins.

ILLUSTRATOR'S DEDICATION:
To Cate, Jamie, and Mingus. Special thanks to Ellen Beier.

Werks Series
www.PTMWerks.com

Published by CurlyQPress
Mansfield, Massachusetts
www.CurlyQPress.com

© 2015 Patrick T. McBriarty
© 2015 Illustrations by Johanna H. Kim

ISBN: 978-1-941216-04-0
E-ISBN: 978-1-941216-05-7

Library of Congress Control Number: 2014954325

Printed in China